THE ATTIC CHRISTMAS

B. G. HENNESSY

ILLUSTRATED BY DAN ANDREASEN

G. P. PUTNAM'S SONS · NEW YORK

HEN/
HOLIDAY

48/22707

Designed by Gunta Alexander. Text set in Centaur.

The art was painted using oil paint on gessoed illustration board.

Library of Congress Cataloging-in-Publication Data

Hennessy, B. G. (Barbara G.) The attic Christmas / B. G. Hennessy ; illustrated by Dan Andreasen.   p.   cm.

Summary: The Christmas tree ornaments are sad when it seems they are not going to be taken out of the attic and hung on the tree one year.

[1. Christmas decorations—Fiction. 2. Christmas—Fiction.] I. Andreasen, Dan, ill. II. Title.   PZ7.H3914 At 2004   [E]—dc21   2001048728

ISBN 0-399-23497-7

1 3 5 7 9 10 8 6 4 2

First Impression

To Kristin, Chuck and Christmas mornings—B.G.H.

For Emily, Bret and Katrina—D.A.

Christmas was more than just one day
in the little white house on Oak Street.
Christmas was a whole season.

The Christmas season always began the weekend after Thanksgiving when the smells coming up the stairs in Grandma Lily's house changed from pumpkin and turkey to gingerbread and evergreen.

When those Christmas smells reached the attic, the ornaments in the green-and-white box knew that soon they would be carried downstairs and hung on the big balsam tree in the living room.

Silver Bell is the oldest. He was given to Lily on her very first Christmas, back when the Christmas tree was lit with candles.

Special Delivery is almost as old. Her tiny tires need to be glued back on almost every year, but the evergreen tree on the back of her truck still has all its needles.

Camel always looks happy with her embroidered smile and shiny beads. When Lily was six, she sewed a tiny present on Camel's saddle with her new sewing kit.

Santa is jolly and fat. Because he is made of glass, Lily hangs him high on the tree, out of the reach of babies and dogs.

All the children in the house have always loved Skier. Though he lost one of his poles many Christmases ago, he is still ready for snow, ready for adventure, ready for Christmas.

Mr. Macaroni, a star-shaped piece of cardboard and silver macaroni, is the only homemade ornament in the box. He was made by Lily's son, Jack, when Jack was in first grade.

Angel is the youngest. With her tiny halo and golden wings, she is Lily's daughter's favorite decoration.

But even in Lily's house, Christmas doesn't last forever. Year after year, on the twelfth day after Christmas, all the decorations are taken down. Lily and her family put them back into their boxes and bring them up to the attic to wait for the next Christmas.

But one year, no smells drifted up the stairs. There were no footsteps in the house.

Finally, Skier opened the box with his pole. "Surely it's almost Christmas, Silver Bell," said Skier. "Why hasn't Lily come to get us?"

"I don't think Lily's coming this year," Silver Bell said quietly.

"Why not?" cried Angel. "Has Lily forgotten?"

"I don't think there will be any more Christmases for Lily," Silver Bell answered.

"But what will happen to Christmas? What will happen to us?" asked Camel.

They all remembered the wonderful Christmases with Lily.

There was Lily's Christmas wedding.

And the Christmases with her children, Jack and Emma.

There was the Christmas Emma fell asleep, still playing with Angel in the new blue dollhouse.

And the Christmas Jack took all of the ornaments for a ride in the snow in his new yellow dump truck.

They all remembered the Christmas of the new puppy.

And of course every Christmas Eve there was Lily, sitting in the big chair, reading, "*'Twas the night before Christmas, and all through the house . . .*"

In the attic darkness each of the ornaments wondered, If there was no Lily, what *would* happen to Christmas?

"It's like the baby with no bed," said Angel.

"What baby are you talking about?" said Mr. Macaroni. "All the babies in this house have always had beds—even the dolls."

"The baby they sing about," said Angel. "The Christmas Baby." She began to sing:

> *Away in a manger*
> *No crib for a bed . . .*

"Don't you see?" she went on. "A baby without a bed. We are ornaments without a tree. This is a Christmas without Santa. A Christmas without presents. A Christmas without a star. A Christmas without bells. Without Lily, there will be no Christmas at all."

"But, Angel," said Special Delivery,
"we have my tree."

"And I have my present," offered
Camel.

"I can still shine," said Mr. Macaroni.

"I can ring!" said Silver Bell. And he did.

"And you have me," said Santa.

"And I have an idea," said Skier.

And so began the attic Christmas.
It was better than no Christmas at all,
but it wasn't the same as the Christmases
they remembered.

It was a Christmas without a family.

Then, one day, Angel heard something.

"There are people in the house!" she said.

Then they heard a familiar voice.

"It's Jack!" cried Camel.

"Surely Jack will come up to get us," said Silver Bell.

"Jack would never forget," added Skier.

"He'll glue my tire on. Jack's always been good with glue," said Special Delivery.

The ornaments waited, but the only people to come up the stairs were the moving men, bringing more boxes to the attic.

The next morning, they awoke to something else.

Mr. Macaroni smelled it first.

"Gingerbread!" he yelled. "WAKE UP, EVERYBODY! I SMELL GINGERBREAD!"

And then the ornaments heard the sound they had been wishing for: Jack and his children, Becky and Mark, coming up the stairs.

"Wow! Look at all this stuff!" said Becky.

"Grandma Lily kept everything," said Jack. "I hope I can find that box of ornaments."

Jack did find the green-and-white box.

But, of course, it was empty. "I'm sure we put those ornaments back in here," Jack said. "Where could they be?"

"Daddy," called Mark.

"In a minute," Jack answered.

"Daddy, I found what you're looking for."

Before you could say "Santa Claus,"
it was a Christmas like the ones they
remembered. There was gingerbread,
evergreen, carols and cookies.

And best of all, Silver Bell, Special
Delivery, Camel, Santa, Mr. Macaroni,
Skier and Angel were part of a family
again.